CLASSIC COLLECTION

ROBIN HOOD

ADAPTED BY SAVIOUR PIROTTA · ILLUSTRATED BY LUIGI AIME

QEB Publishing

How a Young Man Became an Outlaw

On a clear spring morning during the reign of King Henry II, a young man of eighteen was hiking down a path in Sherwood Forest, close to Nottingham. He was tall and strong, with a bow and a quiver of arrows over his shoulder.

Beside the path, several men sat under an oak tree sharing a barrel of ale. There was a joint of meat roasting over a nearby fire. One of the men glared at the boy. He had a thin beard that came to a point under his chin. "And where are you going?" he asked.

"I am on my way to Nottingham," replied the young man boldly. "And who have I the pleasure of talking to?"

"We are the king's foresters," replied one of the other men. "We are looking for poachers who've been stealing the king's salmon from the river."

"The Sheriff of Nottingham has organized a shooting competition," snapped the young man. "I plan to win."

The foresters all burst out laughing. "You're going to beat all the archers in Nottingham?"

The young man's face turned red with anger. "I'll bet my trusted bow that I am a better archer than anyone here—I'll hit the biggest deer in that herd across the glade," he said. He placed an arrow in his bow and pulled the bowstring. The arrow whistled over the men's heads. A moment later, the herd of deer had fled, leaving one in the middle lying on the grass, the arrow sticking out of her side.

"Why, you fool!" cried the man with the pointed beard. "You have killed one of the king's deer. There's a two-hundred-pound reward for catching you now."

"You made me so angry, I did not know what I was doing," retorted the young man. "You are evil, sir, to provoke honest folk to break the law."

The man with the beard rose to his feet. His eyes were bright with rage. "How dare you speak to me like that! I am the Sheriff of Nottingham. I have witnessed your crime with my own eyes, and I shall make sure I claim my reward from the king."

"In that case, sir, you are a crook, for I think you have killed and roasted one of the king's deer yourself," said the young man, pointing to the venison cooking over the fire.

The sheriff turned to his men and hissed, "Get him!"

But the young man was too quick for them. Before anyone had time to draw their sword, he'd turned and fled.

"Let him go," laughed the Sheriff of Nottingham. "We'll get him later. Go to the village and find out who he is. It will be great sport hunting down the little rascal. He'll live to regret the day he called me a crook."

Try as they might, the sheriff's men could not find the young man. They did learn, however, that his name was Robin. His father had been a bitter enemy of the sheriff before he had died. Robin's mother had passed away, too.

Robin Meets a Giant

Robin lived in a manor house with his rich uncle. But now that he was a wanted man, an outlaw, he set up a secret camp in Sherwood Forest. Everyone in Nottingham was talking about it in excited whispers:

"He calls himself Robin Hood. He's gathered together a gang of men, and they rob rich travelers and give the money to the poor," said one man.

"Thank heavens someone is standing up for us poor!" exclaimed a second.

"Even Will Scarlet has joined him. He was Robin's uncle's steward, and a wise man he is," added a third.

Yet someone else said, "They dress in green clothes so no one can see them in the undergrowth. They're all very good with bows and arrows, and swords and staffs, too. And Robin has a horn. Two blasts of it means run away, and three means come to his help at once."

Those three blasts on the horn were heard the very next day, sounding out over the villages around Sherwood Forest. Robin had been on his own when he came to a narrow bridge. On the other side of the bridge was a huge man, more than seven feet tall.

"Stand back, sir," called out Robin, "and let the better man cross first!"

"Then you stand back, sir," growled the giant, "for I am the better man."

"Let me pass or you'll feel one of my arrows between your ribs," replied Robin.

"You speak like a coward," thundered the giant, "for you dare to threaten me with an arrow when you can plainly see I only have a staff!"

"I have never been called a coward before," fumed Robin. "But if it's a fair fight you want, you just wait."

Robin went to a nearby bush and broke off a branch. Then he stripped off its twigs to make a staff of his own.

"Now we are equal," said Robin. "Come on, you big oaf. Let's see what stuff you're made of."

The giant leaped forward, and so did Robin. The bridge shook as they lashed out at each other with their staffs. Robin tried hitting the giant on his back, but the man was surprisingly quick. He grabbed Robin's staff and sent him flying into the stream.

"Is the water cold?" he roared.

"Warm as a tub by the fire," replied Robin, climbing out. He stood on the bank, shaking himself like a wet cat. "You are indeed the best fighter with a staff I have ever seen. What is your name?"

"They call me Big John."

"You don't look so big to me," teased Robin. "I think I'll call you Little John. How would you like to join my band of outlaws in Sherwood Forest?"

"Do you mean Robin Hood's men?" said Little John.

"Aye," said Robin. He blew his horn three times. "And here they come."

From that point on, Little John was Robin's right-hand man.

The Sheriff Sets a Trap

During the next few weeks, the Sheriff of Nottingham sent one man after another to arrest Robin. None succeeded, for Robin was as clever as a fox at escaping, and the local people also helped him hide. The sheriff was extremely worried, for he knew that King Henry himself had heard of Robin and wanted him captured.

One morning, the sheriff announced to his men, "I have it—the perfect way to trap that scoundrel. Listen, everyone . . ."

A few days later, Robin returned to Sherwood Forest from a raid. "I've heard that the sheriff has organized an archery contest at his castle," he told his men. "The prize is a golden arrow. What say we all try to win it?"

"Beware, Robin," said one of his followers, a young man named David of Doncaster. "I have heard from our good friend the landlord of the Blue Boar Inn in Nottingham that it's a trap."

"I'm not scared of traps," laughed Robin. "We'll go in disguise as tinkers, beggars, and friars."

The day of the archery contest dawned clear and warm. A large crowd gathered in the castle grounds. The nobles and the rich people sat on benches; the poorer folk crowded together on the grass behind a fence. Across the grass from the target was a large tent decorated with ribbons where archers were gathering. Most were famous, but a few were new to Nottingham.

The sheriff came out of the castle on a milk-white horse, his lady following on a brown pony. They took their seats on the platform, and the trumpeter blew a fanfare. A knight unrolled a scroll and read out the rules.

"Each archer is to shoot at the target once. The ten whose arrows come closest to the bull's-eye will then shoot another two arrows each. The three who hit the bull's-eye the most will each get another turn. The one of them that hits the mark the closest to the center will be declared the winner. May the best person win."

The archers all took their place behind a line two hundred and forty feet away from the target. As they each shot an arrow in turn, the sheriff examined them. He could see no man in bright green. Had Robin Hood not fallen for the trap?

"There are too many people to see well," whispered the herald in charge of the competition, "wait until there are only ten competitors left."

Eventually, ten people were selected for the next round. They included eight famous archers from the areas around Nottingham, a man in blue who claimed he was from London, and a raggedy old man in bright red with an eyepatch over his left eye.

Neither of the strangers look anything like Robin Hood, thought the sheriff. The man in blue was too tall. The dirty fellow in scarlet had a big brown beard, much bushier than Robin's. He seemed too old, anyway, and was blind in one eye.

A Surprising Winner

"That scoundrel is too much of a coward to come," groaned the sheriff. By now, there were only three left in the competition—two famous archers who were friends of the sheriff and the stranger in scarlet.

"And now," cried out the herald, "which of these remarkable men will hit the center of the bull's-eye?"

The first archer's arrow lodged itself right on the edge of the bull's-eye. The second, named Sir Adam, hit the target right in the center.

"Well done!" cried the sheriff. "I do not see how the stranger in scarlet can improve on that shot."

The stranger took his place and drew his bow, his one eye twitching alarmingly. He took aim. *Zing*! His arrow flew through the air—and split Sir Adam's arrow down the shaft.

"A miracle!" cried Sir Adam to the stranger. "I bow to your skill. No one could beat that."

The stranger was declared the winner. The sheriff rose to his feet and beckoned him forward.

Handing him the golden arrow, the sheriff said to him in a low voice, "Join my ranks. If you hunt down that rogue Robin Hood, I shall make you a rich man."

"Nay, your honor," replied the old stranger. "I do not want to serve any master."

"Then get out of here before I have you thrown in chains, you insolent fool," hissed the sheriff angrily.

The stranger got on his horse and, cheered by the crowd, thundered out of the castle. He stopped only when he was deep in Sherwood Forest. There he took off his eyepatch and false beard, revealing himself to the outlaws who were waiting for him as Robin Hood.

"There, my friends," he said, hanging the golden arrow on an oak branch. "What a fine decoration."

The Sheriff of Nottingham was fuming as he sat down to supper that evening. "All the expense I went to," he said to his lady, "and that coward Robin Hood never even dared to show his face."

As he spoke, an arrow came flying in through the window and lodged itself in the wood of the table. A piece of paper was tied to it.

The sheriff's lady unfolded it. There was a short poem written on it:

> You are the biggest fool
> That ever walked in Sherwood,
> For the golden prize today
> Went to one named Robin Hood.

The sheriff was even angrier to discover that he had been outwitted. He ordered his soldiers to search the entire county until they found Robin and his men.

The outlaws were forced to hide in the deepest part of the forest, living off what they could catch or gather with their own hands.

16

Will Scarlet in Trouble

One morning, Little John said to Robin, "We are running short of food. Can't we find out if the sheriff's men are still searching for us and if it is safe for us to go into the villages?"

"We'll send a spy to the Blue Boar Inn," said Robin. All his men volunteered, but Robin chose Will Scarlet.

Later that day, an old friar entered the Blue Boar Inn. It was full of the sheriff's guards dining on meat pies. The friar took a seat, pulling his cowl low over his face. The landlord approached him. "Ale, good friar?"

"Nay, milk."

"Did you hear that?" laughed one of the sheriff's men. "It's the first time I've heard a man of the cloth turning down good beer."

"And who might you be going to war against with all these swords?" asked the friar.

"We are hunting Robin Hood," came the reply.

Just then, the landlord put a bowl of milk in front of the friar. The tavern cat, smelling it, leaped on to his lap. It slipped, pulling up the end of the friar's robe.

"Why," roared the officer in charge of the men, "I just saw a flash of green cloth under your robe. You are one of Robin Hood's men."

Several soldiers grabbed hold of the poor friar and dragged him out of the inn and off to the castle. He was none other than Will Scarlet.

A Daring Rescue

News of Will's capture reached Robin Hood that evening. "He is to be hanged on the little hill outside Nottingham Castle tomorrow at sunset," the messenger said.

The outlaws pressed around Robin, wondering what to do. "I have a plan," said Robin. "Now, listen carefully . . ."

At sunset the next day, a crowd gathered outside Nottingham Castle. Gallows for the hanging had been built by the great door of the castle. The door opened and out marched a long line of soldiers. The sheriff came next on his horse, protected by chain-mail armor. In his hand he clutched a scroll with Will's death sentence written on it. Then, on a cart, came poor Will Scarlet, his hands tied behind his back.

"Let this man's execution be a lesson to all those who defy me and King Henry!" called out the sheriff.

Will Scarlet seemed crazed with fear. His eyes darted around the crowd, trying to spot a friendly face. And then, hidden under a tinker's hood, he caught a smile. It was Robin Hood. Suddenly, Will spotted more of his friends in the crowd. Alan-a-Dale, David of Doncaster, Arthur-a-Bland! But there were soldiers all around him.

Then the crowd started jostling and pushing forward toward Will. "Stand back!" shouted the sheriff.

A bear of a man leaped onto the cart. "Ahoy there, Will." It was Little John, armed with a small knife.

"Treachery!" roared the sheriff. He pulled on the reins and his horse reared up on its hind legs. The horse pulling the cart backed away from it, bumping Little John and causing the knife to slip out of his hands.

"We need something to cut you free, Will. What shall we do?" asked Little John. He grinned, leaped at the sheriff's horse, and, as quick as lightning, snatched the sheriff's own sword from its scabbard.

Two slashes of the sword and Will was free. Little John threw him over his shoulder and ducked into the crowd. There were three long blasts on a horn and a moment later, men in green were everywhere. The sheriff's men were outnumbered, and before they could do anything, Robin and his outlaws had melted into the crowd.

"Your days are numbered, Robin Hood!" screamed the sheriff helplessly.

His answer was an arrow that went straight through the parchment in his hand!

After the incident at the gallows, the Sheriff of Nottingham became so afraid of Robin that he dared not appear in public. Meanwhile, Robin's gang grew bigger and bigger. Sherwood Forest rang with the sound of their laughter and the clash of their swords as they practiced. The poor blessed their names, for now everyone knew where to turn for help if they were homeless or hungry.

Another Recruit

One bright morning, Robin, Alan-a-Dale, and Will Scarlet were traveling along a country road.

"Who is that coming our way?" asked Will.

"A miller," replied Alan. "He has a mill outside Nottingham."

"That sack on his shoulder must weigh a lot," said Robin. "Let's take it off him."

"But he is poor!" cried Alan.

"We'll only hold him up as a joke," said Robin. "We'll take him into the forest, give him a jolly good feast and fill his purse with silver before we release him."

The three outlaws hid in the bushes, and, when the miller was close enough, they all leaped out.

"Stop, friend!" cried Robin.

The miller dropped his sack. "Who are you?" he asked in a deep, gruff voice.

"We are three hungry men," replied Robin. "Hungry for gold. Give us your gold, friend, and we'll let you go."

"I have no gold on me," said the miller. "I have not a farthing in my pockets."

"Well," said Robin, "we'll help you carry your sack."

"If you rob me, Robin Hood will come to my aid."

"I'm not afraid of Robin Hood," was the reply. "Now come on, let's see what's in the sack. Everyone knows that's where millers hide their money."

"Very well, you win," said the miller. He opened the sack and thrust his hands in the flour.

The three outlaws came closer, eager to see what he would fish out. Suddenly, the miller flung flour in their faces. They reeled back, their eyes stinging.

"Take that, you outlaws!" he cried, and he started thwacking them with his stick.

"Stop, stop," begged Robin. "I am Robin Hood."

"Robin Hood would never steal from an honest miller," said the man, continuing to hit him furiously.

As luck would have it, Little John and some of the other outlaws were close by in the forest. They heard Robin Hood's howls and rushed to the rescue. Little John seized the miller and shook him by the scruff of his neck. "Dare you lay hands on Robin Hood?"

"Leave him be!" cried Robin. He turned to the miller. "You are fierce with a stick, my friend. What is your name?"

"I am Much, the miller's son," replied the other.

"We could do with a man like you in Sherwood Forest," said Robin. "Will you join us?"

A big smile appeared on the miller's face. "That I will," he said, "for there is no glory in grinding corn."

That night, the sound of feasting echoed around Sherwood Forest well into the night, and the smell of roast meat drifted on the air all the way to Nottingham Castle.

Robin Needs a Prayer

One day, Robin said to his men, "We need a good friar, one who will read to us from the Bible and bless us before a raid."

"Then we should fetch the Abbot of Fountains Abbey," said Will Scarlet. "People say he is very holy. Surely, he will not turn away men like us. I would know him, as I saw him at a wedding once."

"Then you, Will, and Little John and David of Doncaster, come with me," said Robin. "We shall go and seek this abbot."

Robin put on a suit of armor, a helmet with a plume, and fine riding boots that he had taken from a knight. "I want to impress the abbot. No doubt he will be dressed in the finest clothes and I want to look just as grand."

The four of them set off, trekking deeper and deeper into the woods, until they came to a shallow river. There was no bridge.

"You did not tell me we had to cross water," said Robin to Will Scarlet. "I would not have come in my boots if I had known."

"You could take them off," said Will.

"Yes, of course," answered Robin. "But I don't want you three laughing at my discomfort. Why don't you rest here? I'll call you when I've crossed the river safely."

Will and the others sat under a tree, and Robin set off, holding his boots in his hands.

Robin is Outwitted

Coming to the other side of the river, Robin heard someone singing. He peeped through the ferns and saw an enormous friar. He had a pie in one hand, a loaf of bread in the other, and a jug of milk beside him.

While Robin watched, the friar started telling jokes to himself and answering in different voices. Robin couldn't help laughing. The friar heard him and, with surprising swiftness, pulled out a sword.

"Who is spying on me in those ferns?"

Robin stepped forward smiling, and said, "I am Robin Hood. I seek Fountains Abbey. Do you know the way?"

"Aye," said the friar. "It is across that river behind me."

"The water looks deep, and I've already crossed one river," replied Robin. "Will you carry me? I don't want to get my finery wet."

"Ha!" spat the friar. "Am I a mule?"

"No," said Robin Hood, "but don't you want to be like Saint Christopher who carried the infant Jesus across a river?"

"You take advantage of my religion," grumbled the friar, "but go ahead and climb on to my back."

They were halfway across the river when the friar suddenly threw Robin Hood into the water. Robin spluttered and struggled to his feet. "Why, you cheat," he growled, drawing his sword. "Defend yourself!"

"Serves you right for thinking you could take advantage of me!" snapped the friar. He whipped out a club from under his robe, and the two lunged at each other in the water. Despite his bulk, the friar danced around Robin and gave him a good beating.

"Do you give up?" he asked at last.

"If you let me blow my horn three times," replied Robin. Robin's horn was answered by his friends, who came running to the rescue.

"Aha," said the friar instantly. "Reinforcements! Now it is my turn to summon help." He put a whistle to his fat lips and blew twice. There was a sudden growling, and four enormous dogs leaped at the outlaws.

"Call them off!" shouted Robin. "You win." The friar blew his whistle again, and the dogs sat down at once.

"Why," said Will Scarlet, "it's my old friend Tuck."

"Your name is Tuck?" laughed Robin Hood.

"Some call me that," said the friar. "And some call me the Abbot of Fountains Abbey, because I live close to a waterfall. That waterfall, sir, is my abbey."

"I told you I knew him," said Will.

"Come and preach to us," said Robin to the friar.

The friar smiled. "On one condition. That you let me join your band of merry men. As you saw, I am a good fighter."

"You will be most welcome," laughed Robin Hood. "Now my band of outlaws is truly complete."

A Wedding Invitation

Before Robin Hood had become an outlaw, he was engaged to marry a beautiful girl named Maid Marian. She was the daughter of a farmer nicknamed Stout Edward. He was rich, and owned land all around Nottingham. But when Robin became an enemy of the sheriff, Marian was sent away to prevent them from getting married.

Now news had come to Robin Hood that Maid Marian was supposed to marry Sir Stephen of Trent, a much older man. Robin was sure that her father had forced her into the marriage, in order to gain favor with the king through Sir Stephen.

Early on Maid Marian's wedding day, Robin Hood and his merry men gathered outside the small church on Sir Stephen's estate. Around it were fields of sheep and cows and a tree-lined brook flowed nearby.

The men hid behind a low wall at the back of the church. Many were dressed as wandering minstrels and entertainers, with musical instruments in their bags. They wanted to see who would be at the wedding.

An old friar came and struggled to open the chapel door with a huge key. Friar Tuck jumped up and said, "Can I help you, brother?"

The old friar smiled gratefully. "What a miracle that you should happen to be passing by, brother."

Friar Tuck managed to unlock the door and the two of them went in.

Not long afterward, wedding guests started to arrive, mostly on horseback. They were followed by men carrying a litter whose passenger was hidden by silk curtains. The curtains were pulled apart and out stepped a bishop, dressed in rich robes and jewels. With him was a priest from a local abbey, whom Robin Hood recognized as a close friend of the sheriff. Last came the bridegroom, Sir Stephen himself, riding a white horse.

The guests filed into the chapel. Robin hissed to his men, "Now, lads, make sure you pretend you are minstrels and entertainers."

The outlaws entered the church with a swagger, smiling and bowing as street performers always do. The bishop asked them to play a song while they waited for the bride. But before they could begin, there was a clatter of horses' hooves outside. A moment later, Stout Edward entered the chapel, with Maid Marian holding his arm.

She looked very upset, glancing around her like a mouse trapped in a room full of cats. Sir Stephen turned to welcome her to the altar, and the bishop advanced with a prayer book wide open.

"Dear people," he began, "we are gathered today to celebrate the holy marriage between Maid Marian and Sir Stephen—"

"Are we?" cut in a voice. The bishop looked around to see the harp player boldly coming forward.

36

An Unexpected Guest

"I don't think the bride is celebrating. She isn't smiling," said the minstrel. "Perhaps this knight is not her one true love."

Sir Stephen reached for his sword, but, this being his wedding day, it was not hanging at his hip.

Maid Marian looked up and recognized Robin and immediately burst into a smile.

"Ah," said Robin. "The bride smiles. I think she sees her real love at last."

"And who might that be?" snapped the bishop.

"It is me, of course, Robin Hood," answered Robin.

And suddenly, the other minstrels threw off their disguises. Robin sounded his horn, and more men rushed in, surrounding the people in the chapel.

Then Robin said to Stout Edward, "I shall be Maid Marian's husband today if she will still have me."

"I never stopped loving you, Robin!" cried Marian. "It is you I want to marry."

"You might have a bride, you scoundrel," thundered the bishop, "but I refuse to bless this marriage!"

"Oh, but I will!" called out a voice from the pulpit. Everyone turned to see Friar Tuck waddling down the aisle.

And so Robin and Marian were married at last, in the presence of a bishop, a priest, a knight, lords, and ladies . . . and Robin's outlaws.

The Sheriff is Worried

A few months after Robin married Marian, King Henry died and his son Richard came to the throne. Richard immediately started a tour of England, to meet his royal subjects.

In Nottingham, he was the sheriff's guest. "I hear talk of a famous outlaw," said King Richard. "His name is Robin Hood."

"He is a most dangerous criminal, your majesty!" spat the sheriff.

"A most interesting fellow," said the king. "He does not rob to become rich himself but to aid the poor. And he does not kill. I hear he has great feasts in the deepest part of Sherwood Forest. Could it be arranged for us to meet this man?"

The sheriff had never in his worst nightmares imagined that the king would want to meet a common criminal like Robin Hood. And he certainly could not run the risk of Robin boasting to his majesty about the sheriff's failed attempts to catch him.

"I hear he is dead, your majesty," he said. "Killed during an ambush this very night."

Robin Hood was not dead, of course. He was very much alive. *But not for long*, thought the sheriff. He had to get rid of the criminal before the king met him. And he knew the perfect person to kill Robin—Sir Guy of Gisbourne, a ruthless knight who would commit the foulest deed for the right amount of money.

A Ruthless Killer

The very next morning, Robin and Little John were strolling down a forest path when they saw a strange fellow dressed in a dark cloak, a hood covering his face. He appeared to be searching for something, looking around him wildly as he made his way through the trees.

"Who might that be?" asked Little John.

"Leave him to me," replied Robin. "You go on. I'll catch up with you when I know what he is up to."

Little John departed, and Robin approached the man. "Good morning!" he called out.

The man pushed back his hood to reveal a scarred face. "Be off, young man. I'm looking for Robin of Sherwood, not a lad in a silly costume like you. Do you know the outlaw?"

"I do," replied Robin. "But, sir, it is you who are silly. Don't you think that Robin Hood has learned of your coming already?"

"Then if he knows, lad, let him come and face me!" cried the stranger. "My name is Guy of Gisbourne, and I have come to speak to him. I hear that he is good with a bow and arrow but that he is lacking in sword skills."

Robin drew out his sword. "Mind what you say, sir. I am Robin, and I tell you I am as good with my sword as my bow."

"Aha! I might have guessed you were him!" cried Guy, and he slashed at Robin with his sword.

42

The sound of clashing steel echoed through the forest as the two men fought. Robin was lighter on his feet than Guy, but the knight was stronger despite his age. Twice Robin felt the tip of the sword at his neck but managed to jump back in time. Then, just as he thought he was starting to win, he stumbled over a root and fell. He saw Guy's sword coming down toward his neck. He reached out and grabbed the blade with his gloved hands. Slowly, he forced it back. Then he kicked Guy's right foot out from under him, and the knight fell on his own sword.

A few minutes later, a voice rang out in the forest. "Sheriff? Are you there?"

"We are here, over by the oak in the clearing," came the reply.

As Robin had guessed, the Sheriff of Nottingham had been waiting with his men. They had caught Little John and tied him to a tree.

The sherriff saw a figure in a dark cloak appear in the clearing. "Is it done, Guy?" he asked.

The hooded figure held up a bloodstained sword. "You have earned your fee," snickered the sheriff. "I have much to celebrate today. Look, we have another of the scoundrels here. We shall drag him to Nottingham Castle and hang him."

"It cost you a bag of gold to get rid of Robin Hood," replied the man in the hood. "It will cost you nothing to be free of this big oaf."

A Royal Pardon

Robin leaped forward as if to stab Little John with his sword. Instead, he slashed the ropes that bound him to the tree. Then he pushed back the hood. The man in the dark cloak was not Guy. It was Robin Hood, who tossed a bow and arrow to Little John.

The sheriff roared like a wounded lion. But an arrow flashed from Little John's bow, and a moment later the Sheriff of Nottingham had fallen in a heap on the forest floor. Dead!

There was a great feast in Sherwood Forest that night. The guest of honor was King Richard. Robin's spies at Nottingham Castle had brought him word of his majesty's wish, and here he was, feasting under the great oak.

"Is this my own venison?" laughed the king. "It is very good. Robin, you are a kind man and a hero to the people. Say you will not poach again and I will grant you a royal pardon."

"Your majesty, I was driven to this life of crime by the Sheriff of Nottingham," replied Robin. "Now that he is no more, it is safe for me to leave the forest but I shall continue to support the poor in any way I can."

"A royal pardon, then," said the king. And he raised his goblet of wine. "To Robin Hood. To fair Maid Marian. And to all Robin's merry men . . ."

About the Author

The legend of Robin Hood has no single author. There were many popular ballads about him in the Middle Ages. There are many versions of the stories about a fugitive, or outlaw, who fought for the poor against cruel rulers in the twelfth or thirteenth centuries. Different writers have retold them in their own way, and Robin Hood has continued to inspire writers and filmmakers up to the present day. The version in this book is based on those medieval ballads still available, as well as on Howard Pyle's very popular novel, *The Merry Adventures of Robin Hood,* published in 1883.

Other titles in the *Classic Collection* series:

The Adventures of Tom Sawyer • *Alice's Adventures in Wonderland* • *Anne of Green Gables*
Black Beauty • *Gulliver's Travels* • *Heidi* • *A Little Princess* • *Little Women* • *Pinocchio*
Robinson Crusoe • *The Secret Garden* • *The Three Musketeers* • *Treasure Island*
The Wizard of Oz • *20,000 Leagues Under The Sea*

QEB Project Editor: Alexandra Koken
Managing Editor: Victoria Garrard • Design Manager: Anna Lubecka
Editor: Maurice Lyon • Designer: Rachel Clark
Copyright © QEB Publishing 2014

First published in the United States in 2014 by
QEB Publishing, Inc.
3 Wrigley, Suite A
Irvine, CA 92618

www.qed-publishing.co.uk

A CIP record for this book is available from the Library of Congress.

ISBN 978 1 60992 470 6

Printed in China